WHERE DOES THE WIND BLOW?

WRITTEN AND ILLUSTRATED BY CINDY RINK

DAWN PUBLICATIONS

To my son Michael,
the boy on the hill.

Library of Congress Cataloging-in-Publication Data

Rink, Cynthia A.
Where does the wind blow? / written and illustrated by Cynthia A. Rink.— 1st ed.
   p. cm. — (A sharing nature with children book) Summary: A mother and son
   share in the universality of the wind, which brushes past people and nature
   all over the Earth and provides a connection between them.
   ISBN 1-58469-040-2 (pbk.) — ISBN 1-58469-041-0 (hardcover)
   [1. Winds-Fiction. 2. Nature-Fiction. 3. Stories in rhyme.] I. Title. II. Series.
   PZ8.3.R4812 Wh 2002
   [E]—dc21
                                                    2002004094

Dawn Publications
P.O. Box 2010
Nevada City, CA 95959
530-478-0111
nature@dawnpub.com

Printed in Korea
10 9 8 7 6 5 4 3 2 1
First Edition
Design and computer production by Andrea Miles

We stand on a hilltop,
you and I,

A tall grassy hill
where the wind blows by.

"Where does it come from?" you ask me,

"Where does it go? What does it see?"

The wind sees children in their beds at night.

It passes people sitting by a campfire light,

It breezes past cows in a buttercup field,

Past a brown bear fishing for her evening meal.

The wind *sees* mountaintops white with snow,

It sings through pine trees in the woods below,

It blows over oceans where sea gulls fly,

Over deserts where the pyramids of Egypt lie.

It whistles through China . . .

Australia . . .

And Spain . . .

It circles round the world and comes back again.

So when you feel the wind blowing on your cheeks and hair,

Remember that wind has been everywhere!

And when the grass stops waving and the wind moves along,

Just think—you and I are now part of its song.

Cindy Rink wrote this book as a message to her son, Michael Allan. As a child he spent a lot of time with his father in New Zealand, while she remained in the U.S. She wanted to capture a sense of connection between them, even from so far away. The wind is a unifying force that everyone feels, around the world; thinking of it like that brought them closer together. Michael's grown now, but the message of love remains as relevant as always. The dog illustrated is Dixie, one of Cindy's several animal companions.

A Few Other Selections for Younger Children from Dawn Publications

The Dandelion Seed and *In A Nutshell* by Joseph Anthony. Both the world travels of a wind-blown dandelion seed and the life cycle of an acorn are simple, sweet stories with underlying metaphors for life.

Stickeen: John Muir and the Brave Little Dog, by Donnell Rubay. This classic true story of John Muir's favorite wilderness adventure transformed the relationship between Muir and a dog.

The Earth trilogy: *Earth & You—A Closer View; Earth & Us—Continuous;* and *Earth & Me—Our Family Tree*, by J. Patrick Lewis. Stunningly illustrated by Christopher Canyon, these books introduce the major habitats in simple, lyrical language, along with the continuity of life and the connections between animals and their environment.

Motherlove, by Virginia Kroll. Animals of many kinds show the qualities of motherhood as they feed, guide, protect, instruct, comfort, and love their young.

This is the Sea that Feeds Us, by Robert F. Baldwin. In simple cumulative verse, this book explores the oceans' fabulous food web that reaches all the way from plankton to people.

Birds in Your Backyard by Barbara Herkert, can help kindle the spark of interest in birds at an early age, portraying common backyard species found all over the North America.

Under One Rock: Bugs, Slugs and other Ughs by Anthony Fredericks. No child will be able to resist looking under a rock after reading this rhythmic, engaging story.

Dawn Publications is dedicated to inspiring in children a deeper understanding and appreciation for all life on Earth. To view our full list of titles or to order, please visit our web site at www.dawnpub.com, or call 800-545-7475.